D0504951

LITTLE   LIBRARY

Sleeping Beauty

AND OTHER STORIES

Retold by Margaret Carter
Illustrated by Hilda Offen

Kingfisher Books

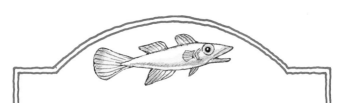

Kingfisher Books, Grisewood & Dempsey Ltd,
Elsley House, 24–30 Great Titchfield Street,
London W1P 7AD

First published by Kingfisher Books in 1993
2 4 6 8 10 9 7 5 3 1

BRITISH LIBRARY CATALOGUING IN PUBLICATION DATA
A catalogue record for this book is available from
the British Library
ISBN 1 85697 079 5

Designed by The Pinpoint Design Company
Phototypeset by Waveney Typesetters, Norwich
Printed in Great Britain by
BPCC Paulton Books Limited

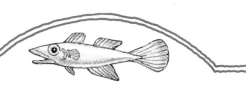

Contents

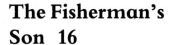

Sleeping Beauty

Charles Perrault

In a land far away where the sun always shines and everyone is happy there lived a king and queen with one baby daughter.

"We must have a splendid party for her christening," said the king and he invited all the kingdom, including the twelve good fairies who lived there, but he forgot to invite the thirteenth fairy, who was not at all good. Far from it!

On the day of the christening all the fairies brought the baby a gift. One said the princess would sing like a bird, another that she would dance like a feather and so on until it came to the thirteenth fairy who, though not invited, had hidden herself behind a curtain.

"The princess will indeed be all that my sisters have said," she said, "but on her sixteenth birthday she shall prick her finger on a spindle and die!" And the wicked fairy vanished.

"The princess shall not die," said a voice and out stepped the last fairy who had saved her gift till now. "Instead she will sleep for a hundred years."

SLEEPING BEAUTY

At once the king forbade anyone in the kingdom to use a spinning wheel and for sixteen years the princess was safe. But on her sixteenth birthday she found a room where she had never been before. And in it was an old woman spinning.

"Whatever are you doing?" asked the princess. "Spinning, my dear," said the woman, who was really the wicked fairy in disguise. "Would you like to try?"

The princess stretched out her hand, and pricked her finger. "Oh!" she cried.

She yawned, rubbed her eyes and fell into a deep sleep. Throughout the palace clocks did not strike, dogs stopped barking, everybody slept. And they slept for one hundred years until a prince came wandering by and found all these people fast asleep. At last he came to the room where the princess lay. "How lovely she is!" he said and bent to kiss her.

She stretched, she yawned, she opened her eyes, the spell was broken!

Then the clock struck, the dog gnawed his bone and the prince and princess stood and watched everyone waking up.

"Welcome, Prince," said the

king. "We'd better send out the wedding invitations!"

"Don't forget the fairies," said the queen. But that bad fairy was never seen again.

The Fisherman's Son

Traditional Caucasian

Once there was a fisherman who caught in his net the most lovely red fish. He had never seen a fish so large. "Look after it for me," he said to his son, "while I fetch a cart to take it to market."

The boy stroked the fish. "You are too beautiful to be taken to market," he said. "You should be free to swim in the sea." And he put the fish back into the water.

Then the fish spoke to the boy. "You have saved my life. If ever you need my help you have only to lift this bone I give you, then call my name and I will come."

The boy took the bone and the fish swam free.

When the fisherman returned to find the fish was lost, his anger was terrible to see. "Go away," he said. "I don't want to see you again." The boy wandered sadly off by himself.

Soon he came to a great wood where he heard hounds barking and through the trees burst a stag with eyes wild with fear.

The boy faced the huntsmen. "Shame on you to chase this gentle creature!" he cried. Then the huntsmen, ashamed of themselves, called their dogs and rode away.

"You saved my life," said the stag. "Take this hair from my coat and if you need me, call my name."

Next the boy saw an eagle attacking a crane. Swiftly he drove away the eagle.

"You saved my life," said the crane. "Take this feather and if you need me, call my name."

Then the boy heard more hunts-men coming and a fox ran to his feet. He picked up the fox and hid it under his coat. "The fox went that way," he told the huntsmen and they rode off.

"You saved my life," said the fox. "Take this hair and if you need me, call my name."

Presently the boy came to a castle. "The princess will marry the man who hides so well that she cannot find him!" he was told.

"Will you give me four chances?" he asked the princess and she said that she would.

The boy took the bone and called the fish. "Hide me," he said. And the great fish took him deep into the sea.

But the princess looked in her

magic mirror and saw him. Then the boy called the stag who hid him in a cave. But again she saw him in her mirror. Next he called the crane who flew with him into the clouds. But again she saw him.

Lastly he called the fox. "Ask for fourteen days," said the wily fox and the princess agreed, for by now she loved the boy.

For fourteen days the fox dug a tunnel until he could hide the boy underneath the princess's room. And there she could not see him.

"Now I will marry you," she said. And among the wedding guests were a red fish, a stag, a crane and a wily fox.

Rumpelstiltskin

The Brothers Grimm

There was once a man who boasted so much about his clever daughter that the king said with a laugh, "I do believe your daughter could even spin straw into gold!"

"Certainly," said the foolish man.

"Then bring her to my palace," said the king.

"But I *can't* spin gold," said the poor girl. "Well, try!" said her father.

The king showed her a room full

of straw. "Spin this into gold," he said and left her. The poor girl wept and wept. She didn't know what to do. Suddenly an elf appeared, to whom she told her troubles.

"What will you give me if I spin the straw for you?" he asked.

"My necklace," said the girl.

"All right," said the elf and he sat down at the spinning wheel. Whistling and singing to himself, he spun the straw into gold. Then he bowed politely and vanished.

The king was delighted to see all the gold and he took her to an even larger room full of straw. "Spin this for me by tomorrow," he said and left her all alone.

Once more she was in despair.

Then the elf appeared. "Help me," she begged. "I'll give you my bracelet if you'll spin the straw into gold." So, whistling and singing, the elf again spun the straw. By morning the room was full of gold.

"Spin for me just one more night," said the king and left her.

That night the elf came again. "I have nothing left to give you," said the girl. "I will spin for you," said the elf, "if when you are queen you will give me your first baby."

The girl thought it so unlikely that she would ever be queen that she agreed and the elf spun the straw.

Next day the king was so glad to see the gold that he made the girl his queen. But a year later when her son was born the elf came again. "Remember your promise," he said.

The queen wept so much that the elf said, "If you can guess my name in three days, you may keep the baby."

For two days the queen tried every name she knew – Tim, Tom, Peter, Paul – but it was none of these. Now she was terribly afraid. There was only one more day left! Then a huntsman came to see her.

"When I was in the woods," he said, "I heard an elf singing this song:

'Today I brew, tonight I bake,
Tomorrow the queen's son I take,

For little knows that royal dame
That Rumpelstiltskin is my
name!'"

The queen knew she had won.
"Your name is Rumpelstiltskin," she
told the elf and in a rage he stamped
his foot so hard he fell through the
floor and was never seen again. And
the queen knew her son was safe.

LITTLE LIBRARY

Red Books to collect:

Beauty and the Beast
and Other Stories

▲

Cinderella
and Other Stories

▲

Goldilocks
and Other Stories

▲

Little Red Riding Hood
and Other Stories